Right Outside My Window

by MARY ANN HOBERMAN
illustrated by NICHOLAS WILTON

For information contact:
MONDO Publishing
980 Avenue of the Americas
New York, NY 10018

Visit our web site at http://www.mondopub.com

Printed in the United States of America

02 03 04 05 06 07 HC 9 8 7 6 5 4 3 2
02 03 04 05 06 07 PB 9 8 7 6 5 4 3 2 1
ISBN 1-59034-194-5 (hardcover)   ISBN 1-59034-181-3 (pbk.)

Designed by John Grandits

Library of Congress Cataloging-in-Publication Data
Hoberman, Mary Ann.
   Right outside my window / by Mary Ann Hoberman ; illustrated by Nicholas Wilton.
      p. cm.
   Summary: While looking outside the window, a child sees something new each day and
   throughout the seasons.
   ISBN 1-59034-181-3 (pbk.) -- ISBN 1-59034-194-5
   [1. Seasons--Fiction. 2. Windows--Fiction. 3. Stories in rhyme.] I. Wilton, Nicholas,
   ill. II. Title.

   PZ8.3.H66 Ri 2002
   [E]--dc21
                                                                              2001055812

There's always something new to see
Right outside my window.

Each day I wonder what will be
Right outside my window.

4

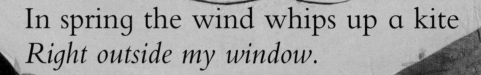

In spring the wind whips up a kite
Right outside my window.

Silver raindrops catch the light
Right outside my window.

Clouds sail in the summer sky
Right outside my window.

A baby bird begins to fly
Right outside my window.

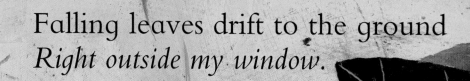

Falling leaves drift to the ground
Right outside my window.

14

A spider weaves her web around
Right outside my window.

18

Snowflakes tumble soft and white
Right outside my window.

The moon shines in
to say goodnight
    Right
        outside
        my
        window.

Summer,
autumn,
winter,
spring,
Right
outside
my window.

What brand new changes will they bring?
Right outside my window.